A MAGIC CIRCLE BOOK

JOEY TIGERTAIL

written by **IRIS TRACY COMFORT**

illustrated by **RICHARD LOEHLE**

THEODORE CLYMER
SENIOR AUTHOR, READING 360

GINN AND COMPANY

A XEROX EDUCATION COMPANY

Joey Tigertail wanted the golden brown horse Tommy Gopher had for sale. Joey thought about her first thing in the morning and last thing at night.

Now as he walked down the road to the cattle pens, he could see her out in the pasture, a lively golden shape. Joey whistled, and the horse with a funny trot all her own came running to him.

"Sihoki doesn't come like that for anyone else, Joey," Tommy Gopher said. "Did you talk to your mother about her?"

"I talked," Joey answered.

Tommy Gopher patted Joey's arm. "I can wait. Today you'll help Dick Osceola. They're moving cattle to another pasture. Do what he tells you and keep out of the way when the men start to work."

As Joey rode across the pasture to Dick Osceola's work party, he was deep in thought. Someday, when he grew up, he would buy his own cattle and be a rancher like Tommy Gopher and the other Seminole cattle owners.

But now his problem was Sihoki. He needed money to buy the beautiful golden brown horse. Tommy Gopher would sell her for $150. That was not much for such a fine horse. But Tommy Gopher was selling her cheap because she didn't get along well with the other horses. Besides, Joey was the only one who could ride her. Sihoki threw anyone else who tried.

Still, $150 was a lot of money. Joey had saved only $50. He tried to think of how long it would take to save the rest.

Then Dick Osceola's shout broke into his thoughts. "Open gates! Lively now!"

After that, Joey was too busy to dream about owning Sihoki and being a rancher. So the time passed quickly and by afternoon his work was finished. Then Tommy let him ride Sihoki for fun. He sometimes did that when there was no more work to do.

Joey and Sihoki were soon racing like the wind toward the line where earth and sky seemed to meet. Then they turned and followed a sea bird flying low over the land.

They had been racing about for an hour when lightning began to flash through the sky. The clouds heaped higher and thunder rolled. Sihoki gave a jog of her head—time to turn back.

Suddenly, as they raced toward the cattle pens, Joey pulled the horse to a stop. Something was moving in the tall grass.

Joey rode over to see what was in the tall grass and found a little girl lost and afraid. Her skin was scratched and she was crying.

Sihoki stood quietly as Joey jumped down and lifted the little girl onto the saddle. Then he swung up in back and held one arm around her. "Hold on," Joey told her softly.

8

The first drops of rain fell as Joey reached the place where Tommy Gopher parked his pickup truck. He found Tommy just getting into the truck and told him about the lost child.

"Where did she come from?" Tommy asked.

"I don't know," Joey answered. "She could have come from the trading store. Maybe her family stopped there to buy something and she wandered away."

Tommy nodded and said, "Get in. We'll take her over to the store and see if we can find her family."

Sure enough, when they reached the trading store, Joey could see some people talking with the owner. Suddenly a woman dashed out and grabbed the child into her arms. She was followed by everyone in the store, all talking at once. Then everyone was quiet as Joey told how he had found the little girl.

12

The child's father introduced himself as Jim
Gareth and said, "I want to thank you with
something more than words."

13

Joey backed away, smiling. Some things you did for money. But to find a lost child—that was not like a job. As much as he needed money to buy his horse, he could not take what Mr. Gareth wanted to give him.

"Words are enough," Joey said. Then he jumped as a cold nose touched his hand. Two beautiful dogs stood looking up at him.

Mr. Gareth laughed at Joey's surprise. "They're Leopard dogs," he told Joey. "Dogs like these are trained to help the cowboys with the cattle. Have you ever seen a Leopard dog?"

"I've seen cow dogs," Joey said slowly. "We don't have any right now, but a lot of the other ranchers have them. The cow dogs I've seen have been just plain dogs. These are beautiful."

"They're not trained yet," Mr. Gareth said.
"So they're not worth as much as they will be
later. Would you take one as a thank-you?"

Joey put his arms around the dog that had
touched his hand. A dog for a thank-you
would be all right.

"This one?" Joey asked.

Mr. Gareth nodded. "Whichever you like," he said. And a short time later the dog was sitting in the pickup truck beside Joey.

As Tommy drove away, Joey looked back and waved to the Gareths. Then he looked down at the dog and said, "I'm naming you Gareth. But we'll call you Gare for short."

"Would you like to train your dog to herd cattle?" asked Tommy. "I can borrow a dog from my friend in Big Cypress and the old dog can help to teach this one."

For the next three weeks Joey spent most of his time training Gare. The dog seemed to know just what a good cow dog should do. He got out ahead of the herd and turned back strays. He obeyed commands such as "Come back!" or "Get behind!" What he didn't know he learned quickly from the older cow dog.

18

Gare never nipped any of the cattle. He never grabbed them by the ear or the nose. He just popped his teeth to show what he wanted and that was enough.

19

Then one day when Joey came to work, he saw a strange car parked near Tommy's pickup. To his surprise, the driver turned out to be Mr. Gareth.

"I was out this way so I thought I'd stop by and see how you're coming with your dog," he said. "I heard you were training him."

Mr. Gareth watched all morning as Gare worked with Tommy and the other men and later as he worked with Joey.

"You're doing a fine job of training him," Mr. Gareth said.

"He's a smart dog," Joey said, pleased.

Gare was earning his keep these days. He was becoming more and more skillful as the weeks went by. Cattlemen often stopped to watch Gare at work. More than one asked if the dog was for sale.

Always Joey said, "No."

20

Then almost before Joey knew it, summer was over and it was time to go back to school. No longer would Joey go to the cattle pens for a day's work with Tommy Gopher and the other ranchers. No longer would he and Sihoki ride the wind. And Gare—who would praise Gare for work well done while Joey was away at school?

Worst of all, his savings weren't enough to buy Sihoki. He could work after school, he thought, and on Saturday. But that wouldn't be enough. Tommy Gopher had waited for so long. It wasn't right to make him wait longer.

On his last day, the day before school began, Joey knew he must have a talk with Tommy Gopher about Sihoki. He went out to the pens before Tommy or any of the other men got there.

As Joey climbed up onto the gate, Sihoki came over and nudged him with her nose. Gare sat down close to him. Joey talked softly to the animals, telling them that the summer with its work and fun was almost over.

At last Tommy Gopher's old pickup came chugging along the cattle road. Mr. Gareth was driving behind the pickup. Joey wasn't happy to see Mr. Gareth. He had wanted to talk with Tommy alone. But he got down off the fence and walked over to Tommy who was now standing beside Mr. Gareth's car.

26

"Mr. Gareth wants to talk with you, Joey," Tommy Gopher said.

"Will you sell your trained cow dog to me?" Mr. Gareth asked. "A Leopard dog that's as well trained as Gare is worth $250 to me."

"No," said Joey. "He's not for sale."

"You still need somewhat more than $50 to buy the horse," Tommy said quietly to Joey. "And the saddle will cost you $100 more."

Joey had to decide what to do. He must give up one thing to get another. Then suddenly he grinned—he had the answer!

Gare was not a pet dog. Gare was a working cow dog. So he must work with the cattle or he would get dull and lazy. He would not be happy staying at home, waiting for Joey to come from school every day. Still, once having owned a Leopard dog, Joey did not want to be without one.

He turned to Mr. Gareth. "I'll sell Gare for $150," he said. "Because Gare will be best off with you. And because I need $150."

Mr. Gareth nodded.

Joey gulped. "But I would like very much to have the first Leopard pup that Gare sires."

"Good," Mr. Gareth said, as he counted out $150 and put it in Joey's hand. Then he put Gare in his car and left with a wave of his hand.

Joey turned and gave the money to Tommy. "I have the rest at home," he said. "I'll get it for you."

"You may as well ride your horse to get it," Tommy said as he took the money.

Joey swung up on Sihoki and suddenly he wanted to shout. But Sihoki would pitch him off if he did such a thing. She didn't like sudden loud noises, not a bit.

And a horse owner had to think of his horse.

DEFGHIJK 765
PRINTED IN THE UNITED STATES OF AMERICA